THE
RAIDERS

To Peter — J. R.
For Margaret Bowgen, with much love — H.C.

This translation has been sponsored by the Danish Arts Council
Committee for Literature. The publisher wishes to thank John Mason for
his work on the translation of this story and the Danish Arts Council for
their generous support.

STATENS
KUNSTRÅD
DANISH ARTS COUNCIL

Barefoot Books
294 Banbury Road
Oxford, OX2 7ED

Translation by John Mason
Graphic design by Graham Webb, Design Principals, Warminster
Colour separation by B & P International, Hong Kong
Printed in China on 100% acid-free paper
This book was typeset in Cleanhouse and Avenir
The illustrations were prepared in watercolour, graphite and collage

British Cataloguing-in-Publication Data:
a catalogue record for this book is available from the British Library

ISBN 978-1-84686-743-9

1 3 5 7 9 8 6 4 2

THE
RAIDERS

Written by Jørn Riel

Illustrated by Helen Cann

Translated by John Mason

Barefoot Books
step inside a story

Contents

1. Life at Stockanæs

The change from winter to spring can be amazingly lovely, especially on Greenland. The days get longer, the air a touch milder, and that great icebound world begins to come alive. First the little snow buntings come, the heralds of spring. They arrive in flocks, often settling near Inuit dwellings to eat the waste they throw out.

Spring was completely overwhelming on the southern part of Greenland, where Leiv and his two Inuit friends had been living with Thorstein Gunnarsson on his farmstead. All of a sudden the light grew so strong that you had to screw up your eyes to stop it hurting. It was a dazzling sunlight that bounced back, reflected by snow and ice. Leiv, coming as he did from Iceland, wasn't used to this much snow. It felt as though he was living in a world made only of ice crystals, and its beauty, which for Apuluk and Narua was nothing special, was a miracle to him. He had never imagined anything could be as beautiful as this Arctic landscape flooded with spring sunlight.

Leiv had been on Greenland for nearly three years now. Even though he missed his family on Iceland now and again, he had no desire to go back home. Thorstein had offered to get him a passage back to Iceland several times, but each time he had thanked him and turned the offer down. He still had so much to discover on Greenland. What he wanted most was to make the long journey up to the region where the Inuit had told him the sun never sets in summer. Shili, the old shaman whose own travels covered immeasurable distances, had told them about this incredible world up north, which was so rich in game that no one would ever need to go hungry.

When the children were found by Thorstein and his men, they were in a pitiful state. Apuluk was worst affected, since the bear they had killed had broken his leg in several places. During those first days he had slept a lot. It was only when his leg really hurt that he woke, looking about him in agony. Then the high fever he was running would make everything around him dissolve and become strangely blurred. But as soon as he could sense that either Leiv or his sister Narua was with him, a calm fell over him, and he drifted off to sleep again.

At the time of the children's arrival a monk called Rollo, sent from the bishop's palace in Gardar, was also living in Thorstein's house. He nursed Apuluk, giving him a herbal mixture to make his fever disappear. He had placed splints along the Inuit boy's lower leg and bound them tight with leather thongs. In the early days, compresses of ice wrapped in bags made of homespun cloth took away the worst of the pain.

Spring was a busy time on Greenland, and still is; for spring brings a renewed energy, inspiring people to catch up with all those things they haven't been able to do over the winter. Now is the time to

tidy up, to rebuild, to hunt and to fill the larder for the winter ahead.

Everyone on the farm helped, from the youngest to the oldest. Even Rollo made himself useful. He went off down the fjord hunting with the men, and despite being small in stature and fragile in build, he was among the best of the hunters. A great animal lover, he would throw a harpoon or shoot an arrow only if he was sure of his target. And he rounded angrily on anyone who just winged an animal rather

than killing it cleanly. Even Thorstein had felt the edge of his tongue on one occasion, when he wounded a seal that then disappeared into the deep, leaving behind a trail of blood.

Rollo never stopped talking. He talked about everything between heaven and the earth – not to mention what lay above heaven and beneath the earth. He told them about the habits of their prey, which he knew almost as well as Apuluk. He spoke about the sea, about the ice, and about what to expect of the weather. When he was alone with Leiv and his two Inuit friends, he often spoke about his God, who was the most powerful of all the gods. And whenever he spoke of his God, he insisted that Leiv should translate his words into the Inuit language so that his friends would understand.

Leiv himself was a Christian, just like his father and his grandfather and his grandfather's father. Before their time, people in the Steinursson clan had believed in the old gods, Thor and Asa, Odin and Freya, and the rest of them, whatever their names were. They could still be called upon to help if for any reason Rollo's God let them down. Narua and Apuluk, on the other hand, were heathens. They believed neither in Rollo's God nor in the old Viking deities. In fact, they had no real gods to turn to at all. Their world was peopled with good and evil spirits. They didn't have to bother about the good spirits, because they were good no matter what. As for the evil ones, they did their best to stay on friendly terms with them.

Rollo was keen to tell the two Inuit about Christ and all his deeds. He told them about the Christians' paradise, which was a place up in the heavens where everything was lovely, and he told them about hell, which lay under the earth and consisted of a great inferno where Satan roasted all those miserable creatures who were not Christians.

Narua shivered each time she heard about hell. She asked Leiv whether he thought it would be safest for her to become a Christian, since she hated the idea of burning down there on Satan's great bonfire. Leiv didn't know what to say. He believed everything Rollo told him, and the last thing he wanted was for Narua and Apuluk to be sent down to hell when they died.

But Apuluk shook his head. 'That little man speaks with more than one tongue,' he said. 'Everyone knows that heaven up there is a cold and desolate place, and that only whingers go there, while under the earth it is nice and warm and there are good hunting grounds.'

'But that's not what Rollo says,' protested Leiv.

'Rollo could be wrong,' Apuluk answered gently. 'He is only a man and cannot know more than a man.'

'But what is God, then?'

Apuluk shrugged his shoulders.

'I guess no one knows. I think God is everything. We Inuit know about Sila. Sila is the weather, the mountains, rocks, grass – everything. That's what I think God is.'

'You don't believe in the great bonfire down there, then?' There was hope in Narua's voice.

'No. I don't believe in that and I don't believe in Rollo's paradise either. I just think that there is good and evil. Old Shili, who is a great shaman, knows most of the good and evil spirits. He has been on journeys to the moon and other places where ordinary people have never ventured. And he's never said anything to us about meeting Rollo's God.'

For a while Apuluk's words set Narua's mind at rest. When he told her about the spirits of the Inuit, she felt unsure about Christ. She knew all about the old stories the Inuit had always told and couldn't really grasp this new God, who lived in a country that people knew nothing about, a place so far away that it was hard to believe it even existed.

'Maybe it's best you keep the God you know,' she said to Leiv, 'and we'll keep our spirits.'

Leiv nodded. He knew how deeply the Inuit believed in their magical spirit world, and he had no wish to force his religion on his two friends.

But the monk did not give up that easily. He kept on preaching to the children, and one day, due in part to his influence, Narua almost volunteered to be baptised.

2. Narua and the Inferno

Over the three years he had lived on Greenland, Thorstein Gunnarsson had built up an impressive farmstead. Its turfed buildings were spread across a wide area of land and had almost become part of the landscape.

There were six buildings in all. Three of these were sheep sheds, two were barns and one a farmhouse, which had the cowshed built onto it. It was a spacious dwelling with many rooms, since Thorstein had a lot of young farmhands, both men and women, and only a few serfs. They all lived in the farmhouse, which was built of brown turfs and flat, grey stone. The roof was covered in grass turfs laid in graceful curves over the thick walls below.

Inside the house there were rooms for all the farmhands, a dormitory for the women, another for the 'unfree', as the serfs were also called, and finally a large bedchamber for Thorstein, his wife, Helga, and their little girl, Frida. There was a large pantry, where the food was kept and prepared, a kitchen area which had an opening in the roof so the smoke could escape, and a large communal living space, where Helga's loom had been erected.

At the furthest end of the house was a small room which these northmen particularly enjoyed using. This was the bathhouse. In the bathhouse stood a large oven built on small boulders, a tub containing water to throw over the heated stone and a massive wooden bench, where everyone could lie and steep their bodies in the scalding steam.

Every Saturday, the fire was lit in the bathhouse. Leiv loved spending time in there, and he often urged Apuluk and Narua to try it. But neither of them really felt like it. The two Inuit had never tried that kind of bathing. When they had a bath, it was always in a small mountain lake, where the water was so cold that it gave them goosebumps and turned their skin blue. So they never had a bath more than once or twice a year.

On Thorstein's farm there was a young bull, which was kept penned in an enclosure behind the main house. The bull had been brought to Greenland as a young calf three years ago, and the long and arduous journey had made it go slightly mad. It had grown into a huge and handsome bull, dark brown, but with long sharp horns and a very aggressive manner. The only person who dared go near it was Thorstein, and even he admitted that it was always with a beating heart and a stout stick in his hand.

One day the bull had managed to ease open the gate to the enclosure using its horns. It got out of the pen and was pacing around, on the lookout for someone or something to attack.

Narua, who had been working in the pantry, was just on her way to the dung heap with a bucket of peelings. And since she was the only thing the bull could see moving, it launched itself at her with a hoarse bellow.

Narua heard the thunder of hooves behind her. Turning her head, she could see the crazed, brown beast coming at her, its heavy head lowered and almost touching the ground. Throwing aside the bucket, she let out a high-pitched scream and leapt for her life. Straight into the muck heap. After a couple of steps she had sunk right up to her knees. Desperate to escape the bull, she flung herself forwards, rolling across the huge and stinking mound.

The bull dug in its forelegs and skidded to a halt, sending stones and gravel flying over Narua. It prodded at the dung heap with one hoof, letting out a deep growl of irritation and feverishly tossing its huge head from side to side. Narua lay there, pressing herself as far into the muck as she could, and so frightened that she didn't even notice the stench that rose up all around her.

How long she lay there she didn't know. Every time she raised her head to look for someone to help, the bull stamped its leg and bellowed furiously at her. With every fibre of her being she hoped that Apuluk

and Rollo would soon return from the shore, where they had gone to turn the fish laid out to dry on the rocks. She knew that she could expect no help from the others who lived on the farm. It was Saturday evening, so they had all retired to the bathhouse.

But then Rollo appeared, on his way to the farmhouse. Lost in thought, he was ambling along, hitting the ground with his stick. The sound distracted the bull's attention away from its prisoner in the dung heap. It turned towards the monk, bellowed a declaration of war and took off at high speed in his direction.

Rollo stopped. He looked around in confusion, threw away his stick and with one mighty leap was up on the low roof of the hay barn. The bull tried to climb up after him, but the overhang of the roof broke away and the crazed beast dropped to the ground again.

Narua now saw her chance to escape. She rolled down the dung heap and raced for the farmhouse, where she ran into Helga, who was on her way out of the bathhouse to rinse herself with cold water from the barrel by the door.

'Goodness gracious!' Helga stared at Narua, aghast. 'Whatever do you look like! And you stink to high heaven!'

Narua pointed towards the barn, where the bull now held Rollo in check.

'Has it got loose?'

Helga gripped Narua firmly by the arm and dragged her through the house. In the living area she pulled off all the girl's clothes. Then she opened the door to the bathhouse and shoved her in.

'The bull's loose!' she said to Thorstein. She was laughing. 'He's cornered Rollo up on the barn roof.'

Everyone in the bathhouse was laughing too. Thorstein got up and went outside. Soon afterwards he came back in.

'Rollo's in no danger,' he said. 'He's sitting up on the roof shouting down at the beast, using the kind of words that should never cross the lips of a man of God.'

He turned to Narua. 'That's an awful stink coming off you, my girl. Give her a good scrub, Helga, so we can get rid of that smell of the muck heap.'

Still in shock after being attacked by the bull, Narua had no recollection of what had happened to her before being taken to the bathhouse. But once the hot air struck her and the thick steam filled her lungs, her head cleared. She gasped in horror and looked about her, terrified.

The huge bench was covered with naked human bodies. She could dimly see them through the steam – saw those large red bodies glistening with sweat, saw the laughter in those inflamed faces, heard a hubbub of voices, all talking at once. Then an arm suddenly reached out for a scoop and filled it with water, which was immediately flung across some large stones. And with a dreadful hissing, the stones threw up a huge cloud of steam under the low ceiling. A fearful heat came over Narua's naked body.

She turned imploringly to Helga, who had begun scrubbing her clean with birch twigs. She was convinced that this room behind the communal living area was the hell that Rollo was always talking about, the place where Satan boiled the heathens alive.

24

'I promise to become Christian,' she sobbed to Helga. 'I will do everything Rollo says.'

But Helga didn't understand what she was talking about. She just smiled and nodded and kept on scrubbing. Then she turned Narua round so that the girl stood facing the door and began scrubbing her back and neck. Suddenly Narua tore herself away. She flung open the door and rushed through the house. At full speed she dashed down the long passage, opened the main door and raced as fast as her legs would carry her round the house. She was totally overtaken by her desire to get away from the hell she had just visited.

Narua kept running, up and over the fell that rose behind the house. She leapt like a frightened hare and didn't stop until she reached the lake where they fetched water for the farm. She ran out into the lake and let the icy water chase the heat of that hellish room out of her body. She was still sitting there, the water up to her neck, when Leiv came running after her. He had been lying asleep on the bench when Helga came in with her and had only half heard her promising to become a Christian.

'What are you doing?' he asked in astonishment. He crouched down by the edge of the lake.

'I promise to be a Christian,' stammered Narua, 'as long as you don't take me back to hell again.'

'Hell?'

'Yes, that room behind the living area.'

Leiv laughed. 'But that's the bathhouse. Did you think we had all gone to hell?'

Narua nodded. She got up and waded towards Leiv. 'Do I have to be baptised now?' she asked anxiously.

Leiv shook his head. 'No, I don't think you do. Baptism is something you choose of your own free will. Maybe it's best you carry on believing in your spirits. Or would you like to be baptised?'

'I'd rather not,' answered Narua. 'But I am very afraid of your hell.'

'If hell is no worse than Thorstein's bathhouse, then I don't think I'd much mind going there,' Leiv said, laughing.

Narua smiled. 'You haven't got any clothes on.'

Leiv looked at her. 'Neither have you. We were in a bit too much of a hurry.' He reached out a hand. 'Come on. Let's go back to the bathhouse and get warm again.'

'Never,' replied Narua. 'Never!'

3. Summer

As the days went by, the sun climbed higher and higher in the sky, and out on the fjord the ice grew soft and dangerous to walk on. The landscape was almost completely clear of snow now, and the short Arctic summer had begun. The fields around the farm were covered in green, and in the turfed walls of the farm buildings grew small tufts of rough grass and many herbs, which Rollo gathered and dried for use in winter.

Over the fell behind the farm a carpet of heather spread a riot of bright colour all the way to the mountains that rose beyond, still clad in snow, and a multitude of flowers thrust up out of the earth – saxifrage, roseroot, crowfoot and poppy.

Summer was in the offing at Stockanæs. Every day, Apuluk was helped out into the sunshine by Rollo, and there he sat for much of the day drinking up the warmth as he cut new arrows for his bow or repaired harpoons and flaying knives for Thorstein's men. Every once in a while, he had Rollo help him down to the shore, where he lent a hand spreading the fish out on the rocks to dry.

Everyone on the farm liked this soft-spoken Inuit boy. They knew that, had it not been for him and Narua, Leiv would not be alive. Without their help, Leiv would have died of hunger and cold when he was washed ashore almost three years earlier when Thorstein's ships were lost at sea.

Narua and Leiv also helped on the farm. Narua was often in the pantry with Helga, and there was no end to her amazement at the strange food the northmen consumed. It was completely different from what she was used to, even though the meat often came from the same animals.

The thing she thought tasted worst was the buttermilk, which Helga prepared every day in the pantry. They called it 'skir'. It was sour and there was absolutely nothing she liked about it.

Leiv, meanwhile, joined in when the men went hunting. But he soon discovered that, compared to the Inuit, these northmen were both slow and clumsy. It was mostly because of their weapons, he felt. These were heavy and unwieldy and no match for those of the Inuit. He tried to teach Thorstein and his people how to use Inuit weapons, and he suggested that they construct light boats made of hide, which were quicker and easier to manoeuvre than the heavy wooden boats they used. But none of the northmen wanted to change their old and well-tried methods.

This meant that it was always Leiv who brought home the biggest catches, and it made Apuluk chortle with joy when his friend's spoils were carried ashore.

The days went by quickly for there was much to do. And before they knew it, half the summer had gone and it was time to gather in the hay and firewood for the winter ahead. They found firewood by collecting heather twigs and driftwood. It was then stacked behind the largest of the sheep sheds alongside large mounds of turf, which the men cut from a nearby bog.

The hay was very important for the northmen. Without it their horses, horned cattle and sheep would die during the winter. So Thorstein and his people scoured the valleys and cut grass. It grew only sparsely here and there, and they often had to walk for a whole day to find particularly good meadows. As soon as the grass was dry – and that happened very quickly in the warm and sheltered fjord – they went round again and gathered in the hay. They could not relax until Thorstein had enough hay under cover to be absolutely certain that the animals would be able to survive the winter, no matter how long or hard it was.

Apuluk grew stronger with every day that passed. By midsummer the monk was able to take off the splints. He rubbed and massaged the boy's wasted muscles every day with his strong, slender fingers, and soon Apuluk could walk on his own with the aid of two

sticks, which Rollo had cut for him from driftwood. Now and again, he would sit beneath the cliffs that rose above the water, and several times he managed to harpoon fish playing unawares in the shadow of a cliff wall.

One day, Leiv spied a longship sailing in along the fjord. He had seen that kind of boat on Iceland, and he knew that they were used for military expeditions to England and Ireland. He shouted to Thorstein, who was standing by the farm's forge. Thorstein came out and looked in the direction Leiv was pointing.

'Are they pirates?' asked Leiv. He had heard that down at East Bay they had received a number of visits from pirates, who had burnt down farmsteads and taken people as serfs.

Thorstein shook his head. 'No,' he said, 'it's Grimur Thorleifsson. He came here once before, shortly after we first arrived. A hard and wicked man, they say, who generally brings trouble with him.'

Rollo came out of the house. He squatted down beside Apuluk. 'Grimur is just coarse and stupid,' he said. 'It's his brother Rane who's the hard and wicked one.'

'But what are they doing here?' asked Leiv.

Rollo shook his head. 'No one can say until they've gone. Maybe they just want to see how we're doing.'

Leiv watched the big ship curiously. 'I've never heard of anyone sailing such a broad-beamed vessel up here,' he said.

'It's true that it hasn't happened for a long time,' answered Rollo. 'But those two brothers are almost always on the high seas. They have been to Norway several times, fought in Ireland and some years ago went on a journey to Markland.'

'But where's their farmstead?'

'To the south,' answered the monk. 'They have settled in a place not far from Gardar. Their great-grandfather took land there. He was a shaman and a chieftain, and one of the last heathens to allow themselves to be converted to Christianity.'

Leiv couldn't take his eyes off the ship. It had unusually beautiful lines. The stern and the prow were covered with intricate carvings; there were many oar holes, and from the well amidships rose a great mast. Loud shouts met his ears and he saw a couple of men haul down the rough striped sail. The other men on board sat on their sea chests, and slowly the ship turned so that the terrifying dragon's head that decorated the prow faced the land.

4. The Visit

Everything that could walk or crawl on Stockanæs was gathered at the landing rock, where the foreign ship lay to.

Narua kept close to Leiv, looking in amazement at the huge, bearded men sitting in two rows, each with his own oar. Struck dumb at the strangeness of the ship and its crew, she gave a sudden start when a giant with a red beard down to his chest leapt ashore, followed by a slim, handsome man strangely dressed in baggy trousers and some kind of anoraq with one sleeve missing.

These were the Thorleifsson brothers, Grimur and Rane. They were inseparable, it was said. Indeed, it was rumoured around Greenland that it was only when they were together that they made a whole person. Grimur without Rane would have no brains, and Rane without Grimur would have no strength.

Narua looked at the pair of them and shuddered. She was reminded of the ships she and Apuluk had seen out at sea off the coast of Simiutat. Now she understood why her father and the others in their group had tried to get as far from these people as they possibly could.

Grimur greeted Thorstein with exaggerated politeness. 'We were passing,' he said in a thunderous voice, 'and fancied tasting the beer at Stockanæs Farm.'

Thorstein smiled. 'Everyone is welcome at Stockanæs,' he said, 'but beer is not something we have in store.'

Rane, meanwhile, said nothing. He stood completely still behind his brother, smiling. He had a dreadful smile, thought Narua, a smile that never reached his eyes. His gaze swept across Thorstein's people and on up towards the barns, which were full to bursting with newly gathered hay.

Grimur turned to his brother, who pointed towards the barns. 'Ah, I can see you have good stocks of hay here at Stockanæs,' he bellowed enthusiastically.

Thorstein looked up at the haystack.

'We have a fair amount, but not more than can be eaten during the course of a winter,' he replied.

'That's a shame.' Grimur shook his head slowly. 'The thing is, caterpillars have eaten our grass and we need to get hay before winter comes.'

'We can spare none here,' answered Thorstein firmly.

Grimur looked round at Thorstein's men. Then he let out a great guffaw, and the men in the ship joined in.

Rane continued to smile. His eyes flicked from face to face until they lighted on Narua, standing half hidden behind Leiv.

He moved swiftly across to her. 'Aha! I see you've caught a Skrælling, Thorstein Gunnarsson,' he spoke for the first time. 'I'll wager she's hopeless as a serf, though, isn't she?'

Thorstein didn't reply. He was keeping a sharp eye on Grimur and the men in the ship.

'We've caught loads of these little people,' continued Rane, 'but we've always had to cut them down to size because of their stubbornness.' He reached out one hand and grabbed Narua by the hair. 'I have a bad habit when it comes to Skrællinger,' he laughed unpleasantly. 'I prefer to see them shorter by a head.'

He wrenched Narua's head backwards and with his free hand felt for the sword at his side. But before he could draw it from its sheath, Leiv was on him. Quick as a flash he drew his long knife and pressed it hard against Rane's throat.

'Let her go!' he shouted furiously.

Rane gasped in surprise. He released his grip on Narua's hair and let his hands fall to his side. That smile never left his lips, however.

Grimur let out a bellow and reached for his sword.

'The further your sword comes out of its scabbard, Grimur,' Leiv yelled at him, 'the deeper my knife goes into Rane's throat.'

Grimur let his hand rest on the hilt. He was growling like a mad dog and staring with bloodshot eyes at Leiv.

Thorstein scowled. 'No one threatens the Inuit at Stockanæs,' he said. 'If that's your brother's way, he is not welcome here on our farm.'

But Grimur made no reply. It was as though he hadn't heard Thorstein. He stood as if turned to stone, one hand resting on the hilt of his sword, the other thrust in under the cloak he wore over his shoulder. He stood before Thorstein, his gigantic frame hiding Leiv and Rane.

One of the men on the ship had slipped over the side unseen. Without anyone noticing, he had crept ashore and was a couple of paces away from Leiv. He now leapt up and raised his axe to drive it into Leiv's back. But before he could deliver the blow, there was a hissing in the air and a dull thud. The man sank noiselessly to the ground, impaled by an arrow.

Grimur came to life. He roared in fury at the sight of the dead warrior. Rane, still held by Leiv, squinted down at the point of the knife that was touching his throat.

'Control yourself, Grimur!' he said, looking into Leiv's eyes. 'We had better set sail again,' he added,

smiling, 'just as peacefully as we came. For we are clearly not welcome at Stockanæs.'

But Grimur was too far beside himself to remain calm. 'Who killed my man?' he roared. 'Where's the coward who killed my best man?'

A clear, high voice came to them from the farmhouse above. 'His name is Apuluk, and God guided his arrow.'

Everyone except Rane and Leiv turned their heads towards the voice. And there, a couple of yards from the main door, stood Apuluk and the monk Rollo. Apuluk had his bow in his hands and a fresh arrow already fitted to the string. The arrow was pointing at Grimur's chest.

'A Skrælling!' burst out Grimur in horror. 'Was my man killed by a lousy Skrælling!' He glared furiously at Thorstein. 'Does Thorstein Gunnarsson now depend on fairy folk to protect him? Have the people at Stockanæs begun to wage war on their own kind?'

Unable to control himself any longer, he drew his sword and leapt towards Leiv. Rane let out a high-pitched scream as he felt the boy's blade pierce the skin of his neck.

But it wasn't Rane's scream that stopped the giant. A second arrow from Apuluk's bow bored deep into the muscle of the arm holding the sword. The weapon fell on the rocks with a clatter, and Grimur was left gasping for breath. He pirouetted once and was on the point of falling. It looked so comical that Thorstein's men began to laugh. With a chuckle Thorstein kicked Grimur's sword down into the water.

Once he had found his footing, Grimur grasped the arrow to pull it out. But it was too deeply embedded and all he achieved was to snap it in two.

Without a word he turned and leapt on board, blood pouring down his arm. He yelled at his men to take up their oars and then turned to Leiv.

'You let my brother go, Leiv Steinursson,' Grimur shouted. 'I know who you are. You are the one who disgraced yourself by letting your father's death go unavenged – you are the one who has become a Skrælling!'

'He can go free,' replied Leiv, 'once he has laid down the sword that deprives the Inuit of their heads.

He came to bring trouble and so must leave without his weapon.'

On Rane's lips the smile faded. To have his weapon taken from him by a mere slip of a boy was a deep disgrace. But he did as Leiv asked. Slowly he let his hand slide down to the hilt of his sword. He looked over Leiv's head. Up by the house Apuluk was still standing, with a fresh arrow fitted to his bowstring, aimed straight at him.

With clenched teeth he let the sword fall at Leiv's feet. He felt the boy take the knife from his throat. 'One day I shall fetch this sword and kill you with it,' he snarled with a hoarse whisper.

'Then you will have to learn to swim first,' laughed Leiv. He put the toe of his sealskin boot to the sword and with a kick sent it spinning out into the water.

'Go,' he said curtly. 'No one here at Stockanæs is afraid of you, Rane Thorleifsson.'

Rane jumped aboard, and the ship slid away from the landing rock, pursued by mocking laughter from the shore. Thorstein's farmhands gloated over the defeat of the two brothers. They looked forward to winter visits from the other farmsteads, when they would be able to tell the story of how the dreaded brothers had been disarmed and shamed by two boys who had seen no more than fifteen summers apiece.

5. Longing for Home

For the two Inuit children, time at Stockanæs seemed to pass unbelievably quickly. Spring had become summer and they had scarcely noticed. There was so much that was new to see and hear and learn.

For Narua, weaving was a great marvel. She could sit for hours as still as a young hare watching the beautiful homespun cloth grow out of Helga's loom. It was miraculous to her that the wool of the strange creatures the northmen called sheep could be turned into something as lovely as the cloth Helga produced.

During the summer, Helga made a dress for Narua as thanks for having taken such good care of little Frida. All day long the child was Narua's shadow. The Inuit girl was never too busy to play with her.

The dress was Narua's most treasured possession. The first time she took it in her hands, she was struck dumb with delight. The dress was very beautiful, she thought, but also very odd and impractical. It was made of two broad pieces of cloth, a front and a back, with a shoulder strap attached to each. Fastened to each shoulder strap was a large broach of some hard material that Helga called bronze. The dress went right down to below Narua's ankles, which made walking in it almost impossible, but she was enchanted by it all the same.

She thanked Helga for the gift by sewing a pair of warm boots out of sealskin that Leiv had brought home from the hunt. She went to great trouble to sew them with stitches that were so fine that Helga would be able to walk in water with them without getting her feet wet.

Narua put the dress away under the plank bed where she slept at night. She loved it but she didn't like wearing it. It looked all wrong on her too – Leiv and Apuluk both split their sides laughing the first time she tried it on. What was more, she thought it was terribly scratchy and stiff compared to well-chewed hide, and it held neither the warmth nor the good smell of clothes made of animal skin.

It was a dress of great value, however. Narua knew this because Leiv had told her that homespun cloth was one of the most important goods the northmen could trade with. They could barter it for costly goods like wood and metal. People everywhere believed that wool from Greenland was the best because it kept its warmth even when it got wet.

For Apuluk, the most fascinating place was the forge. He couldn't believe that Thorstein and his men could use something that looked like earth, something that they found not far from the farm, to create the amazing material they called iron. For a long time Apuluk thought that Thorstein possessed magical powers, like Shili at their settlement, but Leiv told him that iron could be made by anyone once they had learned the craft.

Apuluk's leg was healing fast. He could walk without a stick and, even though he still had a slight limp, he was able to head off with Leiv and Narua into the mountains, where they collected eggs and hunted small game such as grouse or hare. They always took Frida with them on these trips, and the two Inuit soon became very fond of the quiet little girl.

Aged five and mute since birth, Frida was nonetheless bright and quick on the uptake. Apuluk taught her to use a sling, and it wasn't long before she could fire it better than either Leiv or Narua.

One day, on a trip in the mountains, Narua began to talk about her parents and the settlement. She was talking to Frida, who had been listening attentively even though she didn't understand the words.

Narua spoke of the sorrow her parents must feel now that she and Apuluk were gone. She spoke of her little brother, who was so young when they left that he had not even been given his proper name. She talked about the Inuit summer camp, about the huge amounts of meat that they hunted and brought back home, and about her grandfather, who was so good at telling stories about things that had happened long, long ago.

Leiv and Apuluk were listening, too, as they lay in the heather eating the bilberries they had picked.

'Father and Mother must think we're dead,' said Apuluk. 'I'm sure they have looked everywhere for us. They probably found our dogs and think we died on the ice.'

'Well, they haven't looked here,' said Leiv, smiling. 'Do you remember how afraid old Shili was of northmen? And the time he tried to have me killed when you found me after the shipwreck? He thought I was an evil spirit.'

The two Inuit nodded. No, it was very unlikely that their people would dare look for them among the northmen.

'Maybe we should try to find them soon,' said Apuluk. He cast an apologetic glance at Leiv. 'I would like to go home to let them know we're alive. But if you'd rather stay here, Narua and I can make our way alone.'

For a long time Leiv sat looking out across the fjord. From where they were lying, high on the mountainside, he could see down across Thorstein's farm and way out into the fjord. 'No,' he said at last. 'If you leave, I will go with you.'

'But Thorstein and his people are your tribe,' objected Apuluk. 'Wouldn't you rather be with them than with us?'

Leiv looked at Narua thoughtfully. She was lying with her profile turned to him, and her long black hair fell like a raven's wing across her cheek.

'I'm an Inuk,' he replied. 'Inuk means "human", and that is what I am.' He laughed. 'You mustn't think you're the only humans on the earth just because you call yourselves Inuit.'

Apuluk joined in. 'We didn't know there were other humans before we met you northmen.'

Narua turned her head. She looked Leiv straight in the eye, and they smiled at each other. 'Leiv has become like the Inuit,' she said earnestly. 'He belongs with us.'

Apuluk stretched his bad leg. 'I agree. I just didn't want to make it hard for him, if he would rather stay with Thorstein. He mustn't do it for our sake.'

Leiv picked up a small round stone and held it out to Frida. The girl placed it in her sling, swung the leather quickly round her head and let the stone fly. With a faint smack it struck the bag full of crowberries that they had left a little higher up the slope.

'I'll travel with you,' said Leiv, 'for I have no wish to live on this farm for the rest of my life. I want to travel like the Inuit do. And I don't want to part from you two.'

He grabbed his bow and stood up. 'This evening I shall tell Thorstein. He'll understand why we're leaving.'

6. The Departure

By lucky chance, Thorstein had promised to sail Rollo down to the bishop's palace at Gardar. Three years earlier Rollo had been dispatched by Bishop Alf to look after the church's interests in the northern settlements.

One of his duties was to collect taxes for the Pope in Rome in the form of walrus ivory and the long, curling tusks of the narwhal. Everywhere he went he administered Holy Communion. At the Communion service he was supposed to distribute wine, but, since this was impossible to get hold of in Greenland, he brewed an alcoholic drink out of crowberries, which the bishop had been taught how to make by King Sverre of Norway himself.

Rollo's journey in the northern part of the diocese was now over. Everyone at Stockanæs was sad to see the little monk leave, and he himself was very sorry that the bishop wanted him to return home.

While transporting Rollo back to Gardar by sea, Thorstein planned to hunt seal and cod and gather driftwood. This last was very important for the northmen on Greenland because there were no trees where they lived. Wood had to be pulled out of the sea, which had carried it all the way from the rivers of Siberia, or else they had to sail to Markland or Vinland to find it. The northmen had already discovered America some years previously. They had tried to settle over there, for the land was more fertile than Greenland, but constant disputes with the native peoples forced them to return home. However, they still made forays over there to fetch grapes and, above all, wood.

Thorstein made no objection to the children leaving. He understood their longing for home and suggested they sail with him as far as they wished.

He was going to sail round the southernmost point of Greenland, and on the way they would be certain to find traces of their tribe or of other Inuit.

Helga was saddened by the thought of their departure. She had grown accustomed to these three young people and knew that Narua especially would be dreadfully missed by her little daughter. But she also understood why they could not remain at Stockanæs any longer.

As they were leaving, Narua presented Frida with an amulet made from the claw of a raven, which she herself had always worn on a leather thong around her neck. She had been given it by Shinka, her grandfather, when she was born and was giving it to Frida to protect her from evil, just as it had always protected her.

One day in August they set sail from the farm. Half of the men went with them, eager to mix with other people and to hear news of the great world outside Greenland. It was far too long since they had had any contact with the old world up in West Bay. They had heard from Rollo that a few ships from Norway had visited East Bay, but they themselves had received no visitors since Thorstein arrived from Iceland three years earlier. So much was happening further south, in Europe, that people simply did not have time to think about the navigation of Greenland. Rollo had told Leiv that even ten years earlier ships used to come to Greenland once or twice a year.

For three days they sailed, helped along by a stiff northerly wind. They kept as close as they could to the shore, following the towering, broken coastline. The

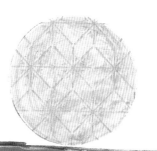

nights were still light, and Apuluk, probably the keenest of the children to reach home, kept watch in the bows of the ship. Day and night he sat staring longingly towards land in the hope of catching a glimpse of an earth house, a tent or a man in a kayak. It was not until the fourth day that his wish was granted. They had just left a wide fjord behind them and were sailing around a string of small, barren islands when he shouted to his sister.

'Narua! Look there, between the islands!'

She looked in the direction he was pointing. 'What is it?' she asked.

'I saw something move. Now it's gone.' Apuluk stood up and went amidships. 'I'm almost certain it was a kayak.'

'Just think if it was Father or someone else from the group!' exclaimed Narua. 'Do you think he saw us?'

'Yes, that's why he disappeared so quickly behind the island. He is frightened of the northmen.'

The two Inuit went astern and explained what Apuluk had seen. Leiv translated for Thorstein. 'I think our group are further to the south,' he said. 'But if you put us ashore here, we can ask these people if they know where Apuluk and Narua's family are.'

'But do you think you'll make contact with them?' asked Thorstein.

'I'm sure we will. They won't run that far away. They'll be lying safely in some good hiding place, keeping an eye on us to see what we do. As soon as they see that we three are alone and that you've sailed on, they'll show themselves.'

Thorstein looked down into Leiv's eager face. He smiled. 'Well, you must do as you wish. I can see that you, too, are keen to get back to your friends. Are you sure that you'll get a friendly reception? It might be a group that you don't know.'

'They are Inuit,' replied Leiv, 'so they'll not harm us.'

Thorstein shook his head and laughed. Leiv trusted the Inuit blindly. Thorstein himself had heard a different story, about northmen killed by wandering Inuit. It was true that these had been acts of vengeance because the northmen had themselves killed 'Skrællinger' and robbed them of meat and skins. But it did at least indicate that these people did not always have friendly intentions.

The three young friends were set ashore on the mainland behind the long string of islands. Thorstein left them some of his provisions. He took each of the children in his arms before they went ashore. Then he turned to Leiv. 'Once there was enmity between us, Leiv,' he said. 'I killed your father as blood vengeance for my brother. You have the right to kill me one day.'

Leiv nodded. 'There is no more enmity between us, Thorstein Gunnarsson. My arm will never grow long enough to kill you. You have righted the killing of my father by being a father to me and to my foster sister and brother, Narua and Apuluk. May there always be peace between us.'

Leiv looked Thorstein straight in the eye, compressing his lips into a thin blue line to stop himself from crying. Then he turned abruptly and leapt down onto the rocks. Rollo thrust his head over the rail.

'Never forget, Leiv,' he shouted, 'that your God goes with you. He is always at your side.'

Leiv, Narua and Apuluk waved as the ship was rowed out to sea. They remained sitting there, watching until the large, square mainsail had been set, bearing the vessel swiftly out between the islands. Leiv rose to his feet, but Apuluk drew him back down.

'I think we should stay here,' he said. 'Just stay and wait. Some time soon the man in the kayak will come looking for us.'

Narua knelt down and drew her stone pot out of its coverings. 'If you light the fire, I'll cook some meat while we wait,' she said. 'And then we'll have something to offer our guests, too.'

Leiv and Apuluk gathered brushwood and twigs, and soon the pot was bubbling cheerfully with seal meat that had been caught from the ship.

Leiv stretched out in the heather again. Lying on his back, he stared up into the unending blue of the sky. How strange life had become, he thought. His early childhood had been spent on Iceland with his father and mother. That had been a wonderful time with no worries at all. He had played with his cousins, trained himself in the use of weapons, helped around the farm and ridden out and about on Flax, his horse. What had become of Flax? Who had they given him to all those years ago after he'd crept on board Thorstein's ship to kill him?

He lay there thinking about his first years with the Inuit. They had taught him to live like an Inuk, taught him to look after himself, to share with others and to live in fellowship. He loved this fellowship, which oddly enough did more up here to bind people together than it did to separate them. If they had made the same demands on other people's property on Iceland, it would have led to violence. Back on Iceland, and for that matter, among the northmen on Greenland too, they had to fight to extract things from each other. But among the Inuit, people made no distinction between giving and taking. Maybe this was because they owned nothing that was superfluous. The only things they knew were their common needs: to eat, to drink, to work, to sleep. It was all so simple, and that was why he liked living with the Inuit. Because their lives were straightforward and full of integrity, and because he felt himself attached by stronger bonds to Narua and Apuluk than to anyone else.

So Leiv lay deep in thought. Narua was sitting staring into the bubbling pot, where the meat twitched and turned convulsively under a thick layer of greyish foam. Apuluk was sitting looking across the strait between the islands in the hope of catching sight of the man in the kayak.

Suddenly they heard a thrumming sound and, before any of them could react, an arrow had buried itself with a thud in the ground no more than a hand's breadth from Leiv's head.

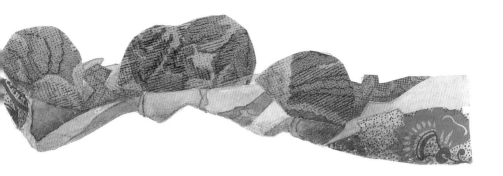

7. With the Inuit

Narua stared at the arrow in disbelief. It had been shot with such force that its tip and almost a third of the shaft were buried in the earth. If it had hit Leiv, he would have been dead on the spot. Furious, she leapt to her feet.

'Since when did Inuit shoot arrows at other Inuit?' she screamed out, stamping her feet on the heather in her rage.

Even Apuluk had got to his feet. He quickly snatched up his bow, setting an arrow to the string. 'Have the people in this part of the Land of Humans fallen under the spell of evil spirits?' he shouted. 'Can you no longer tell the difference between kinsfolk and quarry?'

After a moment's silence a man's voice answered: 'We wish no harm to the Inuit. But the northman boy with the fair hair must die.'

'Show yourselves,' shouted Apuluk. 'The fair-haired boy is an Inuk and my brother.'

Two men stepped forwards from a ledge in the cliff above them. One of them had a huge red scar that went from one eyebrow down over his nose and mouth to his chin. His lips were cleft, which made his mouth appear set in a frightening, contorted grimace.

Apuluk lowered his bow. 'Why do you want to kill the northman?' he asked.

The men approached slowly and tentatively. With their weapons at the ready, they kept glancing behind them as though expecting an attack from behind.

'Northmen are evil,' replied the disfigured man. 'They have killed almost everyone in our group. Therefore they have to be wiped out. As long as they live, there will be discord in the land.'

Narua turned her back on the strangers. 'There is cooked meat,' she said, bending down over the pot.

'Could it be that a pair of hunters newly arrived might wish to please a woman by sharing her food?'

The men came to a halt a few paces from the fire. Leiv sat up and looked them over. The disfigured man held a hand in front of his face so that they couldn't see his scar. The other man was old. Maybe just as old as Apuluk and Narua's grandfather, Shinka. His clothes were dirty and torn, and he looked dreadfully thin.

'It could be that there is a wish to taste your meat,' said the old man, 'now that we have its scent in our nostrils.'

He approached the pot and set aside his harpoon. 'It's a long time since we have eaten seal meat.'

Apuluk nodded. He pointed to Leiv. 'This boy is my brother, and he is more Inuit than he is northman,' he said. 'He was sent to us by the sea, speaks our language and would rather live with Inuit than with northmen. His name is Leiv.'

The man with the scar remained on his feet. For a long time he studied Leiv carefully.

'I have heard speak of a northman boy living in old Shili's group. My name is Pulituk and the old man is

Ukik, and if you are the boy we have heard about, we wish you no harm.' He now came close to the fire and sat down. 'We thought that you were a warrior from the northman ship that sailed to the south. You could have been put ashore to watch over two prisoners.'

'I'm the one who's a prisoner!' Leiv laughed. 'But tell me, Pulituk, how did you get that scar?'

The Inuk removed his hand and let them see the long red cut that split his face in two. 'A northman cut it with his long knife many days ago.'

'A northman?'

'Yes.'

Narua handed the two strangers meat. The old man eagerly grabbed his piece and began to bite into it ravenously. It was easy to see that he had not had a proper meal for a long time. Pulituk ate more carefully, possibly because the hot meat was hurting his cut lips.

'Tell us what happened,' asked Apuluk.

It was the old man who told their terrible story, between large mouthfuls of meat.

'One day we were attacked by a large ship,' he said. 'It was very frightening. At its prow there was a carved head like that of an evil fjord spirit. There were many men on board, and they all carried long knives made of a material that was strong and honed to a sharp edge. We were at a summer camp at the mouth of a fjord we call Isertoq, because the water there is dirty with clay. And we were completely unprepared when the ship suddenly lay to in front of our tents…'

Ukik paused to suck the marrow out of a bone. Then he went on. 'We fought them for a time. Fired all our arrows and threw harpoons and lances. We killed many

northmen. But they were too many for us, and their weapons were designed for battle. They caught all of us Inuit in a big ring and then they started in on the women and children. When they were dead, they struck the heads off the men.'

'But why weren't you killed?' Leiv wanted to know.

Ukik pointed to himself. 'It was my luck not to be at the camp when they arrived. I was out on the water in my kayak and kept myself hidden behind some big rocks down by the shore. They never noticed me, and that was what saved me.'

'And you?'

Pulituk looked at Leiv, his eyes full of grief. 'I was caught in the ring. And I saw a huge, red-bearded man kill my two girls and little boy. Then he grabbed my wife by the hair and slit her throat.'

Narua looked at Pulituk in horror. 'How awful!' she whispered.

He nodded. 'When my wife died, I couldn't stay in the ring any longer. I leapt at the giant, got hold of one of his ears and tore it off. A smaller man, who was as fair-haired as Leiv, lunged at me with his long knife, and he split my face down the middle.'

'And then you ran?'

'Yes, then I ran, because my attack had thrown the northmen into confusion. I ran as fast as I could, and they shot many arrows at me. I was hit by two of them, one in the leg and the other in the shoulder. But neither wound could stop me. I ran up the mountain and knew that none of those flat-footed northmen could follow me.

'All day long I lay up there in hiding and watched them load our skins and our meat onto their ship. It was not until they were right out of the fjord and had set course northwards that I went down to the settlement. There I met Ukik, who helped me bury the dead under stones.'

Leiv stared at the earth in front of him. 'You say the ship had a carved head on its prow?' he said. 'And that one of the attackers was a giant with a red beard? The fair-haired man you mentioned, did he have a smile on his lips all the time?'

'Yes. The fair-haired man was always smiling. He was the most bloodthirsty of them all, and it was he who killed most of the children,' answered Pulituk.

'Grimur and Rane!' exclaimed Leiv. 'You hear that? Grimur and Rane wiped out an entire settlement!'

Apuluk and Narua nodded, Narua shuddering in disgust. She could still feel Rane's hand as he grabbed her hair and pulled her head back.

The man with the scar stared at Leiv in surprise. 'Do you know this killer?' he asked.

'Yes, I have had my knife at the throat of that man with the smile,' replied Leiv. 'And now I regret that I didn't kill him.'

Pulituk traced his scar with a finger. 'The one with the smile is the worst,' he said. 'The giant is just a bad man who kills Inuit as you kill your quarry. But the one with the smile is truly sick. He loves seeing others suffer – that means he is sick. And that is why he has to die.'

Leiv looked across at Narua, who was sitting shaken to the core by the story she had just heard. He thought with horror how her throat could so easily have been slit by Rane.

Then Apuluk spoke again. 'Do you know where my parents are?'

'The last we heard of Shili's group was that they were on their way up to the ice cap to hunt reindeer. They may still be there.'

'Strange,' murmured Apuluk. 'I thought they would be further south.'

'There are too many northmen to the south,' said Ukik, 'so they have tried to get up to the ice cap, where the northmen never go.'

Apuluk laid some twigs on the fire and coaxed it to a blaze. 'If you wish, you can travel with us and live with my kinsmen,' he said.

Pulituk shook his head slowly. 'Thank you,' he replied, 'but I have to find the "smiler" and kill him. He killed my family and will kill other Inuit families if he is allowed to live.'

Old Ukik stuck by his companion. 'I am old,' he said, 'and I have never before wished to kill a man.

But I have seen what these northmen have done to our people, and now I can have no peace unless I use my harpoon to try to quench the bloodlust of this "smiler". I would happily go with you to your kinsfolk, but I have to follow Pulituk, for two men are twice as many as one. And against the "smiler" and his people we need to be as many as possible.'

Leiv leaned forwards and placed his hand on the leg of the disfigured man. 'You'll not be fighting alone against Grimur and Rane,' he said. 'I shall go with you, for I, too, have an account to settle with them.'

Apuluk interrupted him. 'I want these two evil men to die, too,' he said. 'But we shall have to use cunning, or they will be too strong for us. So I suggest that we find my father and that we hold council with the hunters in the group. We may turn out to be many more than us four, or we may not. Either way we will gain the advice of experienced men.'

Pulituk and Ukik took a long time to answer. In the end the old man spoke. 'We have listened and find wisdom in your words,' he said. 'For when the people at your settlement hear of the brutality of these two northmen, they will help us to put them to death. It is an ancient custom among our people that we kill those who have gone mad, to free them from the evil spirits that possess them. We will go with you to your settlement and attend council there.'

And so it was. The children and the two strangers travelled many days and nights before they reached the edge of the vast ice cap, where reindeer were to be found for most of the summer. Chancing on the remains of a freshly slaughtered deer, they followed the tracks of sealskin boots, clearly visible in the clay soil, and before long found themselves approaching the cluster of tents that belonged to what Pulituk had called Shili's group.

8. The Council

Reunion brought great joy on all sides. In the evening everyone in the settlement gathered before Apuluk's father's tent to hear about the children's unbelievable journey.

Apuluk modestly told them what had happened since they had left the settlement in the spring. He explained how the ice on which they had been sleeping had suddenly broken off and begun to drift out to sea. Narua then interrupted, describing how Leiv had tried to swim across to the dogs, how his toes had become frostbitten and how Apuluk had had to cut two of them off.

Leiv then had to show them his foot so everyone could see that he now only had three toes. A young

hunter laughed and called Leiv 'Tateraq' after the kittiwake, the gull that also has only three toes.

That made Narua angry. She scolded the hunter, for she didn't think losing your toes was at all funny. She knew how much Leiv had suffered when Apuluk had cut them off. And she said as much to her family as they sat there in the heather in front of the tent. But old Shinka, her grandfather, explained that they'd called him 'Tateraq' not out of spite, but in recognition of how he had tried to save his foster brother and sister. They were glad that he had lost only his toes and not his life.

That reduced Narua to silence. She bowed her head in shame and mumbled that maybe she had been with the northmen for so long that she had forgotten how the Inuit thought.

Then Leiv told them about Apuluk's fight with the polar bear, though he gave Narua the credit for their lucky escape. If it hadn't been for her, he said, they would all have ended up as food for the bears. And without Narua's help they would never have travelled far enough up the coast for Thorstein's men to find them. Narua had both endurance and courage, he said. He had never met a girl like her before.

Taking it in turns, the children now told them all about Thorstein and Stockanæs. And the Inuit listened. The story they heard gave them quite a different impression of northmen from the one they had created for themselves. For what was being described here were people who, by and large, were just like them. It was only when Narua described the encounter with Grimur and Rane that they started to nod in recognition.

'We have heard tales of these people,' burst out old Shili. 'Two of our children were killed by them out along the coast. We found both of them with their heads cut off. That was why we fled inland, for here there has never been any sign of northmen.'

And now at last it was scar-faced Pulituk's turn to speak. He rose and described the atrocities that Grimur and his brother had committed against his group.

Narua sat with her little brother on her lap and listened to the whole story once again. How people could be so evil was utterly beyond her. She clutched the little boy to her, rocking him in her arms.

Once the hunters had heard Pulituk's tale to its end, there was a long silence. They were deeply moved by Pulituk's description of the horrors that had taken place at Isertoq, and a great anger arose in them against these foreigners. Apuluk's father was the first to speak.

'We have heard much talk this evening,' he said. 'First about these youngsters' long journey, which ended happily with a northman family. Then about these terrible deeds at Isertoq, where many people were killed for no reason.'

He looked around for a moment at the many serious faces around him. Then he continued: 'When I was young, there was a hunter in our group, whose name I will not mention. He was unlucky with his family and with his hunting, and it was as though everything was stacked against him. He wasn't on good terms with Sila, the great unknown that is in everything and which may be the same as the entity that Leiv calls 'God'. And so he began to kill people. First an old hunter and then two other very skilled hunters. Shili tried to drive out the evil spirits that had possessed him, but his power was not strong enough. And so we decided that he had to die. We killed him and bored a small hole in his forehead, so that all that evil could escape through it. I propose that we do the same with these two killers, whom you call by the names of Grimur and Rane.'

He looked from face to face. And he understood that his proposal had been accepted.

'We have always wanted to rid this land of northmen,' said Shili the shaman, 'because we thought they were evil spirits. When Leiv came to us out of the sea, I wanted you to kill him. But he has proved himself and he is an Inuk. Now we know that there are good northmen and bad, and that they are ordinary people, just people from a distant land.'

He cleared his throat and sat rocking gently backwards and forwards. It seemed as though he had to cast about for his words somewhere deep inside himself. Finally he continued: 'Here is one who is now old and without the power to drive these evil people away. But a long life has taught me much, and from that I give you this advice. Rise up and kill these evil brothers.'

Shili had spoken and the Inuit spent the rest of the evening devising a plan. Those who knew about Grimur and Rane explained where their farm lay, and that there were many warriors and a number of women and children living there. Two hunters could describe the farm and its buildings, saying how only a few days ago they had had to hide in the ice because a large ship with a carved head on its prow had sailed from the north into the fjord where the farm was located. So the brothers were very likely still at home.

Before the Inuit lay down to sleep, they had decided on their plan of action. First they would take the inner route and travel to Thorstein's farmstead to make sure that all was well there. Apuluk's father wanted them to leave the very next day, for Leiv had grown anxious on hearing that Grimur and Rane had passed by Stockanæs fjord only a few days earlier.

When Leiv lay down to sleep, he felt Narua lying close beside him.

'Leiv?' she whispered.

'Mmmmm.'

'You must kill Rane.'

'Yes.' He felt for her hand and took it in his own. 'I shall kill him,' he murmured sleepily.

Narua lay looking at him as he slept. It was only when she became aware of Apuluk watching her with a smile that she herself lay down and pulled her hood over her head.

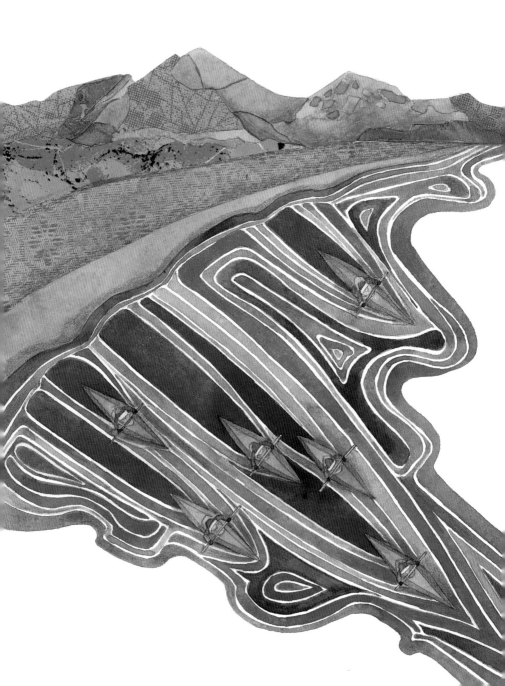

9. Back to Stockanæs

The following morning the men left camp. Armed with bows, harpoons and spears, they walked down to the shore, where their kayaks were concealed in a deep cave.

Narua had gone up the fell with her little brother in her amaut, the extended hood of the anoraq where Inuit carry their babies. She could feel his small, warm body against her bare back, and she hoped against hope that the luck of the hunter would be with the men and that Grimur and his brother would be put out of action for good.

It took a whole day for the Inuit and Leiv to reach their kayaks. They wasted no time sleeping but after packing the kayaks with weapons and provisions for the journey, immediately pressed on out of the fjord so they could reach the outlying shoreline as soon as possible. From there they could follow the course of the northmen's ship across the sea.

They arrived in the early hours. The sea lay spread out in front of them like a vast grey plain in the soft moonlight, and far away they could see a dark line of field ice slowly being pushed northwards.

The long kayak trip had left Leiv and Apuluk exhausted, so they were both grateful when Apuluk's father and some of the older hunters decided to pitch camp. The night passed peacefully. They had posted watches, but neither northmen nor Inuit sailed past. They stowed their weapons and supplies back in the kayaks, and after a solid meal of meat they continued on their journey.

They travelled for four days before Stockanæs loomed out of the evening light. Leiv saw at once that something was wrong. The place was strangely lifeless. No animals in the fields, not even the mad bull, no smoke from the chimneys and not a soul in sight.

When they came ashore, they found the barns empty and most of the hay gone.

'Someone has plundered the farm while Thorstein is away,' Leiv said to Apuluk.

They then went up to the farmhouse, followed by the scar-faced Pulituk. Leiv opened the door and, as he stepped inside, almost fell over one of Thorstein's farmhands. The man lay just behind the door with a deep wound in his chest. Behind him lay two more men, also dead.

They walked from room to room. Everywhere they found the bodies of the dead. Even Helga hadn't been spared. She lay, fatally stabbed, in front of the chest where she kept wool for her loom.

Leiv broke down. He wept until his whole body was shaking. Putting an arm around his friend's shoulder, Apuluk led him outside where Leiv collapsed on the grass, the tears still coursing down his cheeks.

Apuluk sat down at his side. 'Grimur and Rane?' he said.

Leiv nodded his head.

'We must bury the dead under stones,' said Apuluk.

Leiv rose and dried his tears. Then the two boys went into the house again and together carried Helga's body outside.

During the course of that long, light northern night, the Inuit and Leiv buried the many victims of the two brothers. They dug down to the bare rock, placed each body in its own grave and covered it carefully with flat stones so that wild animals would not be able to reach it.

Leiv and Apuluk were placing stones on the grave of one of the serfs when they heard a faint shout from one of the Inuit.

'What is it?' asked Apuluk.

'There was something moving, up there on the fell,' replied the hunter. 'Right up there by the riverbed above the farm.'

'It's probably an animal,' said Apuluk.

'Or a person!' Leiv was screwing up his eyes and looking up towards the river. 'Let's go up and take a look.'

Apuluk put down the stone he had been carrying. Then he began to climb the fell, moving here and there seemingly at random as though scouring the ground for something. Leiv crept away from the grave and round behind the barn, intent on reaching a gully without being seen, from which he would be able to climb the outcrop above it. Back at the farm, the Inuit carried on their work and paid no attention.

After a while they heard a scream. Apuluk, who had reached the river, stopped in his tracks and looked up. High above his head stood Leiv holding a young girl by the hand. In his other arm he held a child, clinging tightly to his neck. It was Thorstein's little daughter, Frida.

With her was Sølvi, a young girl no more than sixteen years of age whom Thorstein had brought with him from Iceland. Her parents had been serfs, and Helga had bought her from a large landowner on Iceland so that she could bring a nursemaid with her to Greenland.

Sølvi was a serf, destined to spend her life serving others. But she was treated well at Helga's and did not seem to feel the burden of her serfdom. She was a pretty and cheerful girl with long plaits, blue eyes and dimples in her cheeks when she laughed.

When Leiv came down from the fell with Sølvi and Frida, she told them what had happened at Stockanæs. And Leiv translated for the Inuit.

They had seen Grimur's longship coming, she said, and Helga had known at once that they were intent on avenging themselves for the humiliation they had undergone on their previous visit. Before the ship lay to at the landing rock, she had ordered Sølvi to run up into the mountain with Frida and to stay hidden no matter what happened at the farm. When Thorstein returned, she would be able tell him about the brothers' visit.

Leiv asked how long it had been since Grimur had been there, and she answered that he had left only three days ago. From the outcrop she had seen the brothers and their men drive off the cattle and horses. She had seen them carry the hay out of the barns and load it on the ship. They had killed all the free men and women on the farm. The only people they had taken away with them were serfs.

Sølvi sobbed as she told them everything that had happened, and Leiv did his best to comfort her.

'We are on our way to find the two brothers and kill them,' he said. 'You must stay here on the farm until we return.'

Sølvi looked at him in horror. 'I don't dare stay here,' she whispered. 'Take me with you, Leiv. I'm afraid.'

'Afraid? Afraid of what?'

'I don't know.'

She looked across at the graves, and Leiv understood. He spoke with Apuluk's father and suggested that Sølvi and Frida should accompany them to the outlying coast. There was an island he knew with a cave where they could shelter. They would be safe there until they could be picked up by the Inuit on their way home.

When they had slept a few hours, they tied four kayaks together in two pairs, and Frida and Sølvi were each given a place on a double deck. They then paddled out of Stockanæs fjord.

As planned, they dropped the two girls at a small island just a few hours' journey from Grimur's fjord.

Apuluk left some provisions and made a fire for them in a small cave, while the men collected brushwood so that Sølvi would have enough to keep the fire going for several days.

'We'll be back before long,' said Leiv. 'You needn't be afraid, for you are safe here. No one can see the

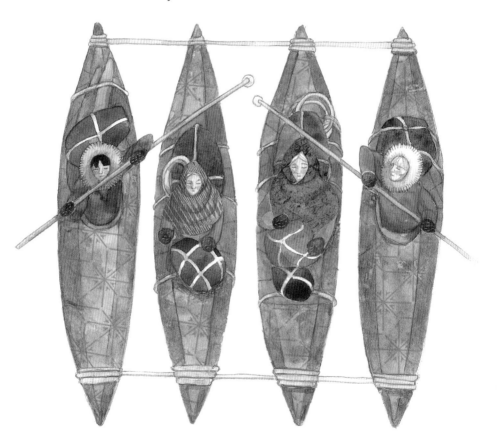

smoke from outside because it is light day and night, and as long as you make sure it burns with a clear flame, no one's going to know there's a fire anyway.'

Sølvi looked at him earnestly. 'But what if you don't come back?' she asked.

Leiv smiled encouragement. 'We'll be back,' he replied. 'Some of us may be staying in Grimur's fjord but not all. You can bet your life on that.'

Sølvi gripped Leiv's hand. 'May God be with you!' she said softly.

'Thank you,' answered Leiv. He looked across at Apuluk, who was standing watching them. 'We have both your God and my God with us, Sølvi, but we also have the many good spirits of the Inuit.' He bent down and lifted Frida up.

'You be a good girl now and do everything Sølvi says,' he said. 'We'll soon be coming back to get you, and then together we'll find your father.'

Frida nodded. She tried to say something, but as always all that came was a hoarse sound in her throat. Once Leiv had set her down, she ran over and wrapped her arms around Apuluk's legs. Embarrassed, Apuluk crouched down and put his arms around her.

'She misses Narua,' said Sølvi.

Leiv nodded. He was thinking that he was missing her, too.

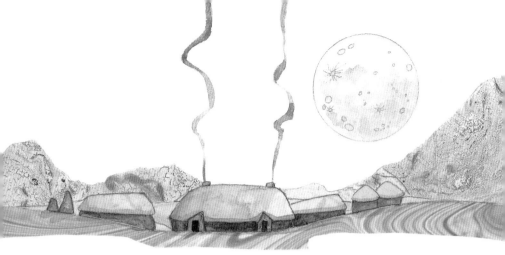

10. The Raid

The little fleet of kayaks reached Grimur's fjord on the afternoon of the same day. Here they pitched camp, now only a few hours from the farm. Having carried the kayaks up into hiding in a gully some way up the mountainside, they lay down to sleep for a few hours in preparation for the fight ahead.

They were woken by the watch when the sun was no more than an orange glow in the west. Without taking the time to eat, they slipped into their kayaks and set off further down the fjord. The narrow channel was full of drift ice, and when they caught sight of the buildings of Grimur's farm, they stayed hidden behind the large floes. The farm was no more than a stone's throw from the shore, and, seeing the smoke coming from the chimney, Leiv could tell they must have a night fire burning in the oven.

At a sign from Apuluk's father, they spread out in their kayaks. They were looking for places along the shore in the shelter of the steep bank that jutted out over the water, where they could creep in fairly close to the longship, which lay half beached on the shingle. The tide was in at the moment, and Leiv could see that when it went out again the ship would be left high and dry and it would be almost impossible for Grimur and his men to put to sea.

Leiv and Apuluk kept close together. They reached the shore at the same time, noiselessly beached their kayaks and crawled behind a boulder that gave them a view of the longship.

'There's a guard astern,' whispered Leiv, 'and there's one up by the house. I hope your father's seen them.'

Leiv let his gaze pan across the shore and up towards the house. It was impossible for him to make out a single Inuk. It was as though they had melted into the ground.

Apuluk couldn't help smiling. 'Inuit know how to make themselves invisible,' he whispered back. 'Otherwise we wouldn't have been able to live by catching seals for all these generations.'

Before he had finished speaking, they heard a rattling noise. They looked towards the ship and noticed that the guard had changed position. He was now sitting slumped forwards as though asleep.

'As long as he doesn't wake up,' whispered Leiv.

Apuluk shook his head. 'He'll never wake again. Look at him properly.'

It was then that Leiv noticed the guard was bent double, his hands gripping the harpoon that had impaled his body.

The guard up at the house had stood up and was looking down towards the ship. He was about to take a step forwards when an arrow struck him with terrific force. He teetered for a moment, swaying from side to side. The guard opened his mouth to shout but all that came out was a faint groan. Then his legs gave way and he sank to the ground with a dull thud.

Only then did the Inuit become visible. They crept swiftly up towards the buildings, and Leiv and Apuluk set off after them. At a harpoon's throw from the house the Inuit halted, then suddenly vanished again. No matter where Leiv looked, he could see no sign of them. He lay down in the heather and waited.

The fire came suddenly. As if by magic, two arrows sped from somewhere below the house, with clumps of burning grass bound around their shafts. One of them buried itself in the roof, where the fire spread in the dry turf, and the other struck the woodwork by a window, which immediately caught fire.

It wasn't long before they heard noises from the house – first a few thuds and, soon after, loud shouts. A man came running through the main door but immediately fell with an arrow in his chest. Another followed close behind, falling before he reached the threshold. The men behind them leapt back into the house to avoid the Inuit arrows.

But they were no longer safe in the house either. The fire continued to gnaw mercilessly through roof

and walls, sending its suffocating smoke down on top of those who were still inside. Then a voice shouted from one of the window openings.

'Let us out! Then we can make it an honest fight!'

'That was Grimur,' said Apuluk.

Leiv nodded. He put his hands to his lips and shouted back. 'They say you love death by fire, Grimur – or is that your brother Rane?'

It was Rane who replied. 'Let the women and children escape, Leiv Steinursson.'

'They can get out on one condition, that you go with them,' answered Leiv.

Shortly afterwards they heard Rane's voice again. 'I am coming with them – to kill you, Leiv Steinursson.'

Leiv called out to the Inuit, telling them to let the women and children out of the house unharmed. When they came in sight in the doorway, he saw a slim, fair-haired man in the middle of the cluster, and he assumed it was Rane. Apuluk grabbed him by the arm.

'It isn't him!' he burst out. At the same instant there came a frustrated shout from the scar-faced Pilituk, who like Leiv thought they'd found the "smiler".

'Watch out!' shouted Apuluk.

He leapt up and drew his bowstring. Suddenly women and children were being brutally flung aside, and Grimur and some of his men stormed out through the door and down towards the Inuit. The evil giant was bellowing with rage, while froth was foaming round his mouth and down his long red beard.

The Inuit shot their arrows almost as one, and a whole swarm buried themselves in Grimur's chest. But nothing seemed able to stop the monster. Yelling like a maniac, he stormed down the slope towards his attackers. At that moment Apuluk's father leapt up. With icy calm he placed himself in Grimur's path, ducked the flashing sword and thrust his spear deep into the giant's body, with such force that the shaft of the spear broke off in his hands. Grimur continued for a few staggering steps before letting out a terrible bellow and falling forwards on the ground.

Grimur's men stopped in their tracks when they saw their commander fall. They turned and began to run back towards the house. But not one of them made it. One after another, they succumbed to the arrows and harpoons of the Inuit.

Leiv raced towards the farmhouse. He shouted to the women to take shelter in the barns and tried to fight his way into the burning building. But the heat in there was too great and drove him out again.

'Where's Rane?' he cried.

'He is not among the dead,' replied Pulituk, who had been looking through the heaps of fallen northmen. 'Maybe he's hiding in the house.'

'Impossible!' Leiv looked in through the door. He could see huge flames exploding in the corridor. 'Let's ask the women.'

They went across to the barn, where the women were standing, clutching their children close, terrified at what might be in store for them. They all knew what Grimur and Rane had done to the Inuit, and none of them expected to be spared. There were four free women, all wives of men closest to Grimur. And there were six serf women, two of whom had been stolen from Thorstein.

'Where is Rane?' Leiv asked a large, muscular woman standing at the front of the group.

She looked at him furiously. 'There's no one by that name here,' she snapped.

'Was he among you when you ran over here?'

She shrugged. 'Maybe you think he's a woman,' she replied with contempt. 'You think a warrior would run away from battle and hide among the women?'

One of Thorstein's serf women came up to Leiv. 'He was among us when we ran over here,' she said. 'He was hiding between the free women.'

The big woman came over to her and hit her across the mouth. 'Shut up, you stupid cow!' she hissed. Again she hit her, so that the blood ran down the girl's chin.

Leiv pushed her away. 'Leave her be!' he shouted angrily. He looked down into the serf girl's face. 'Where is he hiding?' he asked.

'He crawled up through the hole in the hayloft,' she answered. 'Maybe he's trying to hide on the mountain.'

Leiv translated what she said for Pulituk, who nodded in satisfaction. 'If he's taken to the mountain, I'll find him all right,' he said. 'He won't get far there.'

Now one of the other free women stepped forward. 'I know where he is,' she said. 'If you spare the children, I will tell you.'

'Neither you nor the children will be harmed,' said Leiv. 'Now where is Rane?'

'Behind the outcrop above the farm, there's an inlet jutting from the fjord. Rane has a small hut there with a little boat moored alongside. He'll probably be trying to get away in it.'

Leiv looked at her. 'What's your name?' he asked.

'Thorhilde,' she replied. 'My husband was Grimur's steward. We were forced out here to the farm to work for the brothers.'

'Thorhilde,' said Leiv, 'we will harm none of you, I swear it. People will come from other farms to fetch you. But first we have to find Rane.'

Outside the barn, Leiv explained to the Inuit what the woman had said. 'Pulituk and I will go after Rane,' he said. 'Please make sure you do nothing to harm the people in the barn.'

'We came here to heal, not to harm,' replied Apuluk's father.

Apuluk laid a hand on Leiv's arm. 'I'll go with you,' he said.

'But it's not easy for you to run with that bad leg of yours,' replied Leiv.

Apuluk smiled back. 'I can manage well enough,' he answered.

When Leiv turned to call Pulituk, he found that he was already on his way up the mountain. 'Come on!' he yelled to Apuluk, and the two friends ran after him.

From the ridge of a rocky outcrop they could see a tiny, narrow inlet that cut inland far beneath them. Way below them, near the shore, a small turfed hut caught their eye. In the water in front of the hut lay a little boat with a mast.

'He's running down there – look, I can see him!' shouted Apuluk breathlessly.

'Where is Pulituk?' cried Leiv in reply.

'Maybe he ran the other way,' said Apuluk. 'We have to stop Rane before he reaches the boat!'

They started to leap down the rocky mountainside as fast as they could. Suddenly Apuluk stopped in his tracks. He crouched down and then called to Leiv. 'Pulituk's dead!' he cried.

Leiv ran over to his friend. He looked down at where Pulituk's body lay, almost sliced in half by a powerful blow to his back.

'Rane must have been lying in wait behind those big stones and hit him from behind, the coward,' fumed Leiv. Turning away from the body, he looked down the slope. Rane was nearly at the hut, moving swiftly and not yet aware of his two remaining pursuers.

Fury gave wings to Leiv's feet and he almost flew down the mountainside. But he wasn't quick enough.

A wave of despair hit him as he saw Rane slip into the hut and reappear with a large sail in his arms. The sound of stones sent cascading down by Leiv made Rane look up. He threw aside the sail, drew his sword and let out a loud guffaw of laughter.

'Aha, here comes that Skrælling Leiv Steinursson. Welcome, boy! Come on down and get your hair dyed just as red as my dead brother's beard.'

Leiv skidded down the slope, coming to a halt only a couple of paces from Rane. He drew his knife from its sheath. 'This blade once pressed against your gullet, Rane Thorleifsson,' he snarled. 'Now it's itching to get to know you once more.'

Rane lunged at Leiv but he dodged quickly out of reach. He knew it would be hard for him to beat this battle-hardened fighter with nothing but a knife. But he also knew that he had to kill this evil monster. Greenland would never be safe while Rane still lived and breathed.

That incessant smile was playing around the man's lips. He had lost his helmet, and his thick fair hair stood up like a halo around his head. Certain of victory, he laughed and again made a thrust at Leiv.

The boy took a couple of steps backwards to avoid the blow, but one of his feet caught against a stone and he stumbled, lost his balance and fell over backwards.

In a flash Rane was onto him. Leiv lunged out frantically with his knife and buried it in Rane's thigh just as the man's sword came hissing down towards him.

'Now you are going to die!' yelled Rane savagely, his blade hovering above Leiv's head. The smile around his mouth had become an ugly grimace as he lifted his sword to deliver the death blow. Leiv shut his eyes, convinced he was about to die. The thoughts raced through his head in one great confused whirl: his home on Iceland; sailing with Thorstein to Greenland; the Inuit who had become his friends; and Apuluk and Narua, whom he'd never see again.

Leiv waited for what seemed like an eternity, then cautiously opened his eyes. To his astonishment he saw Rane's arm had sunk loosely to his side. He watched him sway, heard a strange rasping sound and only then caught sight of the arrow buried in his adversary's heart. Leiv rolled quickly away as Rane finally collapsed and breathed his last.

Kneeling by the body, Leiv looked back at the mountainside. And there, strolling towards him, was Apuluk, waving with his bow.

'He's dead!' shouted Leiv.

'But of course,' replied his friend.

11. Home Again

Their goal achieved, the Inuit set off back home. As Leiv had promised, they picked up Sølvi and Frida from the island where they had left them and brought them back to the Inuit settlement. They would have to stay for a while with the Inuit until Thorstein returned from Gardar.

Everyone was relieved at the way things had worked out. Even though they regretted killing so many people, they knew it was necessary to get rid of Grimur and Rane. Sølvi was much admired for her beauty and her sunny temperament. She was always cheerful and life at the settlement seemed to suit her well.

Frida became everyone's pet. The old shaman Shili was so taken with the little girl that he offered her a place in his tent. He soon regarded her as his own child and, following the Inuit custom, wanted to adopt her. But Leiv stood firm.

'She has a father,' he said to Shili. 'When he returns, she will have to be with him.'

Shili shook his head vigorously. 'Some have seen what others cannot see,' he said. 'The man who is her father is out on a vast ocean. It may take him several years to find his way home.'

Leiv was aware that shamans often knew more than ordinary people. 'But he is alive?' he asked anxiously.

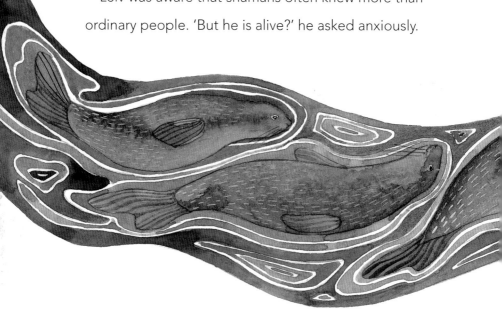

'He is alive,' answered Shili reassuringly, 'but he is travelling towards places unknown, from which he may never return.'

Shortly after their return, the hunters held a council once again. It was high time they found a winter settlement, and there was lively discussion as to whether they should move south to their previous winter site or whether they should head north to find a new one.

'As you know,' said Apuluk's father, 'there are many northmen to the south. Rumours of the killing of Grimur and Rane may reach the ears of these people,

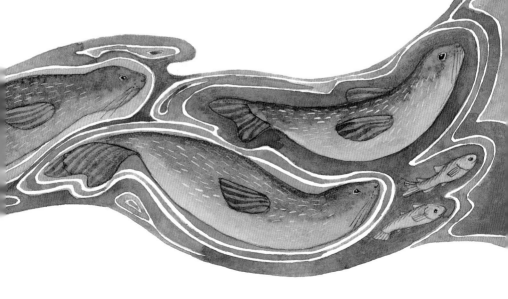

and they may not understand why the Inuit killed the brothers. We want to live in peace with everyone, and therefore I propose that we head north, where there are no people from other lands.'

None of the other hunters raised objections to this. They all wanted to avoid further hostile relations with the northmen. Besides, it would be exciting to find new hunting grounds. It was therefore agreed that they would leave their summer settlement as soon as possible and sail north along the coast to find a new site.

That night Narua, Leiv and Apuluk lay together in the large family tent.

'Are you coming with us to the new winter site, Leiv?' asked Apuluk.

'Yes, of course I am.'

'Don't you ever want to go back to your own people, then?' Narua raised her head and looked at Leiv questioningly.

'All people are my own people,' answered Leiv. 'And what's more I've had an idea.'

'What?' she enquired.

'Well,' explained Leiv. 'You've heard of these two countries that the northmen call Markland and Vinland.'

Narua nodded. 'We heard of them before you,' she said. 'They're spoken of in our old sagas. They are the countries where the Erkiliks live.'

'Yes, I know. And that's what made me realise that you maybe don't even need to sail across the sea to get to them. The Inuit must have been in these countries or else they wouldn't be able to tell stories about them.'

Leiv sat up and looked round eagerly at his two friends. 'I think that, many years ago, the Inuit were driven away from Markland and Vinland to Greenland. If we travel north and keep going in the same direction, I believe we could reach a place where the countries divide. Maybe the sea we know is just a vast great bay. And from the innermost point of the bay you can drive your sled on southwards along an unknown coast to end up in Markland.'

Apuluk shook his head with a wry smile. 'It's not hard to tell there's still a good portion of northman in

you,' he said, 'for such a weird thought would never occur to an Inuk. What do you want to go to those countries for?'

Leiv looked at him in amazement. 'What for? Because it would be an adventure. It would be fun to see whether you could get there without sailing.'

Narua plucked bashfully at the reindeer skin lying across her stomach. 'If you want to go on a journey like that,' she said, 'then I'll come with you. For without a girl you'll never manage to look after your skin clothing properly.'

Apuluk stretched out next to them. 'You're crazy, the pair of you,' he sighed. 'But if you go, I'd better come along too, to make sure you don't get into trouble.'

Leiv lay down again. He closed his eyes and was soon asleep, visited by exciting dreams of a long journey through unknown lands.